and the Pirates

CARAMEL TREE

Caramel Tree is the registered trademark of JLS, used under license.

Series R1000

Word Count : 1,200 words

© JLS 2011 All rights reserved, including the right of reproduction in whole or in part in any form. Exclusive rights by JLS for manufacture and export.

No unauthorized photocopying

No part of this publication may be reproduced, distributed or transmitted in any form or by any means, electronic, mechanical, including photocopying, recording, or otherwise, or stored in a database or retrieval system, without the prior written consent of the publishers as expressly permitted by law, including, but not limited to, in any network or other electronic storage or transmission, or broadcast for distance learning.

Published by JLS

ISBN 89-6629-066-3

Printed and manufactured in Korea

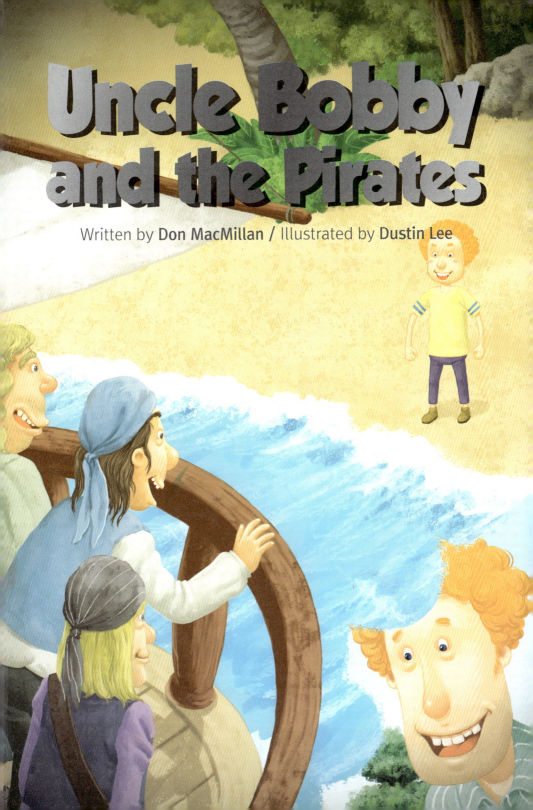

Uncle Bobby and the Pirates

Written by Don MacMillan / Illustrated by Dustin Lee

Chapter 1
The Pirates

"Being a pirate would be a fun job," I say. "But also, a little scary."

Uncle Bobby laughs. "Did I ever tell you about the time I was a pirate?"

"Really?" I look at my uncle to see if he is joking. "I thought you were a lawyer."

"Now, I'm a lawyer. But when I was the same age as you, Tony, I was a pirate – for a short time," says Uncle Bobby.

"Is that true?" I say.

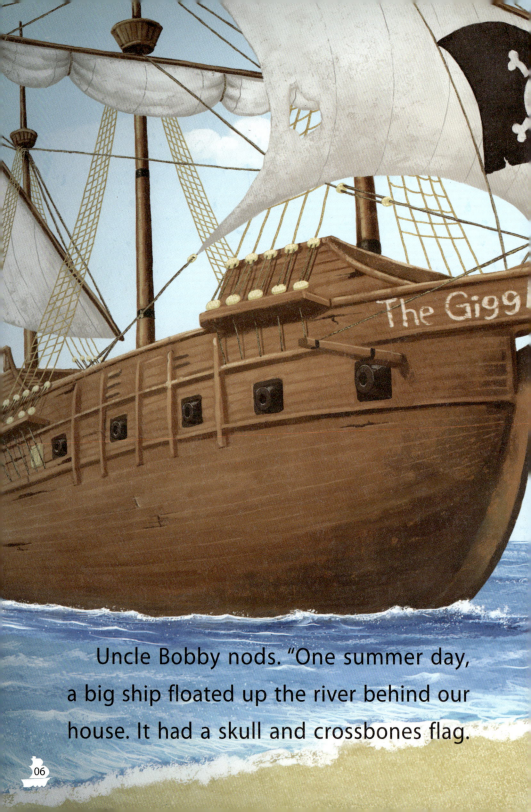

Uncle Bobby nods. "One summer day, a big ship floated up the river behind our house. It had a skull and crossbones flag.

The Giggle was painted across the front. I hid behind some trees and watched it sail into Pirate's Cove."

"What did you do then?" I ask.

"Well, I went to speak with the pirates. I asked them if I could go with them," Uncle Bobby says.

"What did they say?" I ask.

"They looked at me and said I was too small." Uncle Bobby opened his eyes wide.

"Oh!" I say. "How big were you?"

"About as big as you are now," he says.

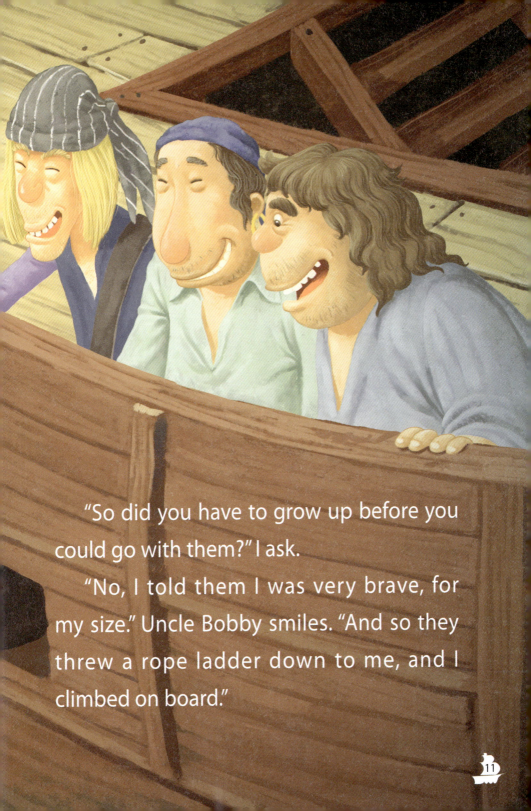

"So did you have to grow up before you could go with them?" I ask.

"No, I told them I was very brave, for my size." Uncle Bobby smiles. "And so they threw a rope ladder down to me, and I climbed on board."

Chapter 2
Captain Candy Tickle

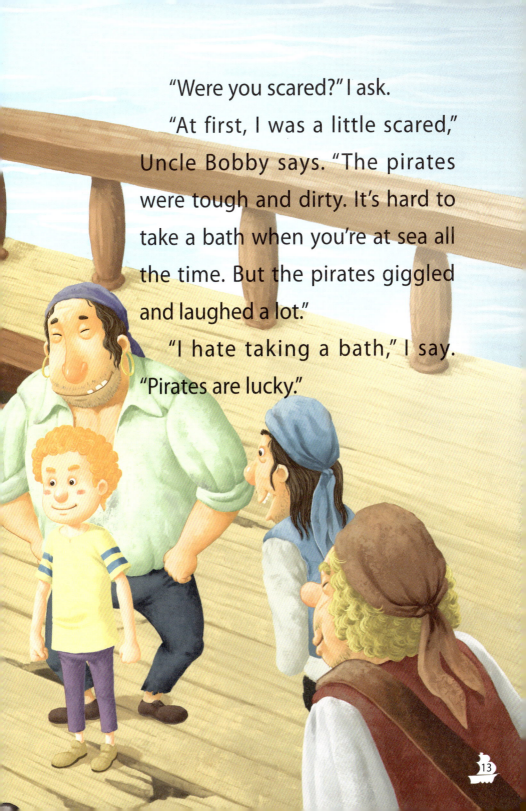

"Were you scared?" I ask.

"At first, I was a little scared," Uncle Bobby says. "The pirates were tough and dirty. It's hard to take a bath when you're at sea all the time. But the pirates giggled and laughed a lot."

"I hate taking a bath," I say. "Pirates are lucky."

"Did they give you a job?" I ask.

"I had an important job," Uncle Bobby says. "Only, instead of a sword, Captain Candy Tickle gave me a feather from his green parrot."

"Why was he called Captain Candy Tickle?" I ask.

"He had a giant sweet tooth, and he was the most ticklish person I've ever met," Uncle Bobby says.

I jump away before he starts to tickle me. "I don't like being tickled at all."

Uncle Bobby laughs. "But Captain Candy Tickle wanted people to tickle him. At first, I used the parrot feather to tickle him under the chin. He only laughed a little. So I tickled the bottoms of his feet with the parrot feather."

I shiver. "I would hate that. Did his feet smell?"

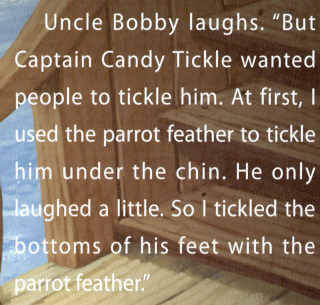

"The smell was horrible. But Captain Candy Tickle gave me bubblegum," Uncle Bobby says.

"What flavor was the bubblegum?" I ask.

"It was cinnamon bubblegum to help take the horrible smell away," Uncle Bobby explains.

"Oooh! I don't like cinnamon," I say. "Did Captain Candy Tickle laugh?"

"Well, he laughed so hard, he fell off the bench and into the ocean." Uncle Bobby laughs.

"Were you in trouble?" I ask.

"Almost. The water was full of hungry sharks. One of them ate Captain Candy Tickle's big hat. The other sharks swam in circles all around the captain."

"Did you save him?" I ask.

"Yes. I threw some of my cinnamon bubblegum into the water. The sharks loved to chew cinnamon bubblegum even more than they loved to eat pirates. While the sharks looked for the bubblegum in the water, I threw the rope ladder over the side of the ship. Captain Candy Tickle climbed back on board," Uncle Bobby explains.

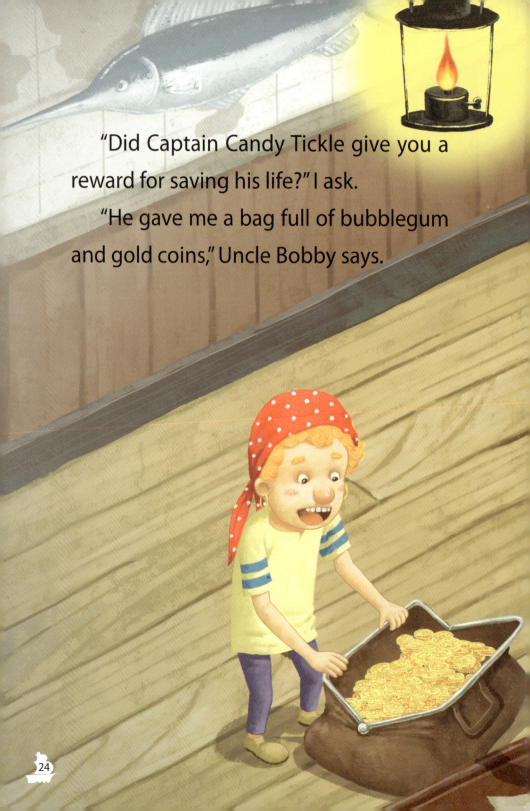

"Did Captain Candy Tickle give you a reward for saving his life?" I ask.

"He gave me a bag full of bubblegum and gold coins," Uncle Bobby says.

"Why were you a pirate only for a short time?" I ask.

"Well, after the rescue, we were hungry. Captain Candy Tickle dried himself off, then started to cook supper."

"What did he cook?" I ask.

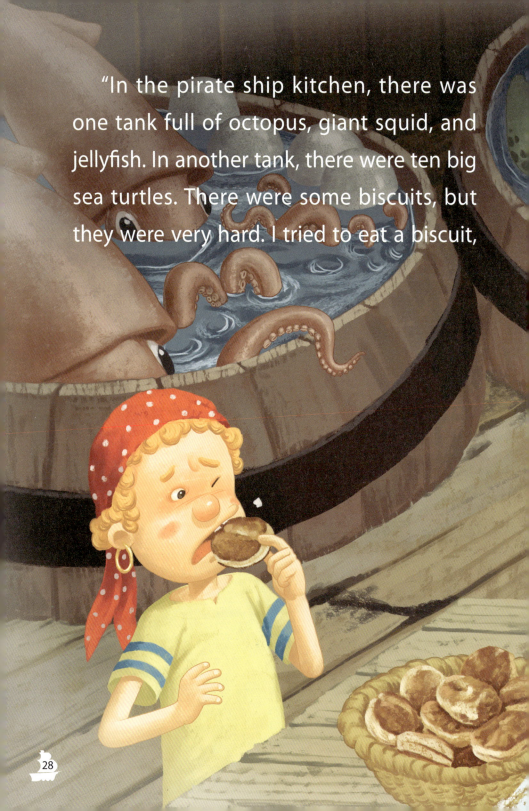

"In the pirate ship kitchen, there was one tank full of octopus, giant squid, and jellyfish. In another tank, there were ten big sea turtles. There were some biscuits, but they were very hard. I tried to eat a biscuit,

but it broke my front tooth." Uncle Bobby shows me his broken front tooth.

"Was that all? No hamburgers? No chicken fingers? No salami pizza with extra cheese?" I ask.

"That was exactly what I wanted to know. But when I asked Captain Candy Tickle, he said, 'My boy, where would we find a cow or a chicken in the middle of the ocean? Pirates only eat seafood and eggs, sea turtle eggs.'

Then he picked up three sea turtle eggs. He popped two in his mouth and offered me one."

"Yuck! Did you eat it?" I ask.

Uncle Bobby shakes his head.

"What did you eat for dinner?" I ask.

"Captain Candy Tickle made a raw squid and jellyfish salad with seaweed and an octopus curry."

"Yuck," I say. "Did you eat those things?"

"I tried to eat the octopus curry, but the tentacles stuck to the inside of my mouth," Uncle Bobby says. "That was when I decided the pirate life wasn't for me."

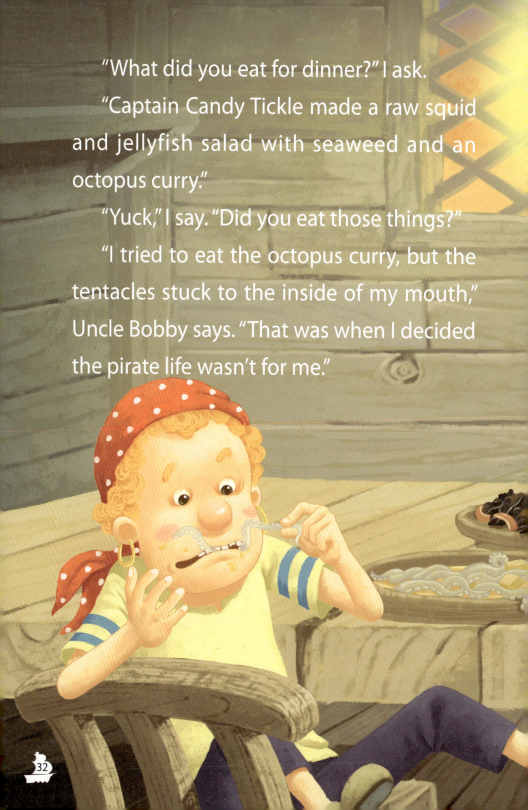

"Did Captain Candy Tickle let you go home?" I ask.

"Well, he didn't want me to go. He said I was the best tickler pirate ever on board *The Giggle*.

There was no way he would let me go home," Uncle Bobby says.

"How did you get away?" I ask.

"I had to escape in the middle of the night. I jumped on one of the sea turtles and sailed away."

I try to imagine Uncle Bobby riding on a sea turtle. "Were there sharks?" I ask.

"Oh yes, there were plenty of sharks. But I gave them cinnamon bubblegum so they didn't bother me," he says. "Until my bubblegum was all gone!"

I gasp.

"What did the sharks do when you had no more cinnamon bubblegum?" I ask.

"The sharks were mean and scary, but they had to bite the turtle before they could bite me," Uncle Bobby says.

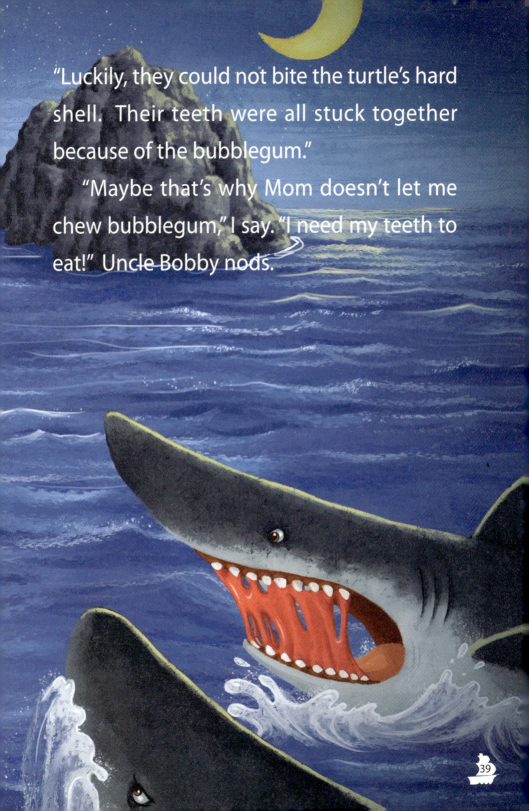

"Luckily, they could not bite the turtle's hard shell. Their teeth were all stuck together because of the bubblegum."

"Maybe that's why Mom doesn't let me chew bubblegum," I say. "I need my teeth to eat!" Uncle Bobby nods.

"Are you hungry?" Uncle Bobby changes the conversation. I nod my head. "Hamburger Palace, here we come!" he says.

"I changed my mind," I say. "I don't want to be a pirate now."

"What would you like to be?" Uncle Bobby asks. "A cook?"

"Nah. I think I'd like to be a dinosaur guy," I say.

"Did I ever tell you, Tony, about the time I saved a T-Rex…?"